BIGGEST NAMES IN SPORTS

KRIS BRYANT

BASEBALL STAR

by Marty Gitlin

FOCUS
READERS

WWW.NORTHSTAREDITIONS.COM

Produced for North Star Editions by Red Line Editorial.

Photographs ©: Matt Slocum/AP Images, cover, 1; Kyodo/Newscom, 4–5; Pat Benic/UPI/Newscom, 7; Ian Johnson/Icon Sportswire/Newscom, 9; Seth Poppel/Yearbook Library, 10–11; Larry Goren/Four Seam Images/AP Images, 13; Lenny Ignelzi/AP Images, 14; Charles Rex Arbogast/AP Images, 16–17; Mike Janes/Four Seam Images/AP Images, 19; Joseph Sohm/Shutterstock Images, 21; David Durochik/AP Images, 22–23; John Fisher/Cal Sport Media/AP Images, 25; Benny Sieu/AP Images, 26; Red Line Editorial, 29

ISBN
978-1-63517-039-9 (hardcover)
978-1-63517-095-5 (paperback)
978-1-63517-197-6 (ebook pdf)
978-1-63517-147-1 (hosted ebook)

Library of Congress Control Number: 2016951017

Printed in the United States of America
Mankato, MN
November, 2016

ABOUT THE AUTHOR

Marty Gitlin is a sportswriter and educational book author based in Cleveland, Ohio. He has had more than 100 books published, including dozens about famous athletes.

TABLE OF CONTENTS

CHAPTER 1

WORLD CHAMPS

The Chicago Cubs were one out away from making history. The 2016 World Series had reached Game 7. A win over the Cleveland Indians would give the Cubs their first championship in 108 years.

Chicago third baseman Kris Bryant had played a big part in the Cubs' success.

Kris Bryant watches his home run leave the park in Game 6 of the 2016 World Series.

The team won a league-best 103 games in the regular season. In the **playoffs**, they beat the San Francisco Giants and the Los Angeles Dodgers to reach the World Series.

But the Indians weren't going down without a fight. Game 7 went back and forth. By the end of the sixth inning, the Cubs had a 6–3 lead. Then the Indians scored three runs in the eighth inning to tie the game. The ninth inning ended without any more runs. The teams would need extra innings to break the tie!

Chicago scored twice in the 10th inning to take an 8–6 lead. But the Indians had one last chance. With two outs, the

Bryant smiles as he slides to the ground after making the final play of the 2016 World Series.

Indians scored a run and had a man on first base. That's when Bryant stepped up to make a play Cubs fans will be talking about for years.

Cleveland batter Michael Martinez hit a slow roller toward third base. As Bryant ran forward to field the ball, a huge smile crossed his face. He knew he was going to make history. He picked up the ball and fired it to first baseman Anthony Rizzo. Martinez was out. The Cubs were world champions!

COMEBACK KIDS

Cleveland won three of the first four games in the World Series. That meant the Cubs had to win the final three games or the Indians would win the series. Bryant hit a big home run to help his team win Game 5. He hit another in a Game 6 blowout victory.

From left, Rizzo, Bryant, and shortstop Addison Russell celebrate the Cubs' Game 7 victory.

After 108 years, the Cubs had finally delivered a World Series title to their loyal fans. And their confident young third baseman helped make it happen.

CHAPTER 2

LEARNING FROM THE BEST

Kris Bryant's father, Mike, played only two years of minor league baseball before retiring. But Mike did receive batting lessons from Ted Williams, perhaps the greatest hitter in baseball history. Mike passed on Williams's words of wisdom to his son as they practiced around their home in Las Vegas, Nevada.

Kris Bryant was a prep baseball star at Bonanza High School in Las Vegas.

Kris developed a **competitive** spirit as a child. Sometimes it got the best of him. When he lost a home run contest to an older boy, Kris returned to the dugout and started crying.

The young Bryant continued to pound baseballs over the fence as he matured. But he also grew into a complete hitter. Kris batted an amazing .447 in three seasons at Bonanza High School. He also embraced learning. He earned straight A's throughout his high school career, except for one B in math.

Bryant was selected by the Toronto Blue Jays in the 18th round of the 2010 Major League Baseball (MLB) **draft**.

Bryant took his powerful swing to the University of San Diego in 2010.

In college, Bryant worked hard on his fielding as well as his hitting.

But Bryant chose to play at the University of San Diego instead. He batted an impressive .365 as a freshman. Even so, he was not satisfied. He went back to work on his swing and became a first-team **All-American** as a sophomore.

The next year, he slugged 31 home runs in only 228 at-bats. After dominating college pitchers for three years, Bryant was ready to see what he could do at the next level.

FAMOUS FRIENDS

Bryant and Washington Nationals slugger Bryce Harper knew each other as kids. They played on the same youth baseball team together in Las Vegas when Harper was seven years old and Bryant was nine.

CHAPTER 3

SOARING TO STARDOM

The Chicago Cubs had the second overall pick in the 2013 major league draft. They chose Kris Bryant. Experts considered Bryant the best college hitter available. He could hit home runs anywhere from the left-field corner to the right-field corner. His bat speed allowed him to hit the fastest of fastballs.

Bryant smiles as he is introduced to the Chicago media in 2013.

17

He played well at third base. And Chicago scouts knew that Bryant worked hard to be the best player he could be.

The Cubs tried to be patient with Bryant. They placed him in the lower levels of the minor leagues so he could adjust to professional pitching. But he soon began a fast climb through the

FAMILY TIES

Kris is not the only Bryant with baseball talent. His older brother Nick batted .417 in his senior year of high school. He also played one season of fall baseball at the college level before deciding to focus on his education. Nick soon became a student at the Massachusetts College of Pharmacy.

Bryant runs the bases for the Tennessee Smokies in a 2014 minor league game.

Cubs' system. He destroyed pitching at every level. He batted .336 in the lower minor leagues in 2013. And he slammed a combined 43 home runs while playing for the Cubs' top two minor league teams in 2014.

Bryant also made a point of giving back to people in his hometown. He spent time signing autographs for fans in Las Vegas. He visited sick children in the hospital. He even paid for new uniforms for the Bonanza High School team. He remained humble and **selfless** even though he was on his way to stardom.

Long-suffering Cubs fans, whose team had not won the World Series since 1908, called for Bryant to be promoted to the big leagues. But the Cubs remained patient. After pounding major league pitching in spring training, Bryant was sent back to a minor league team in Iowa to start the 2015 season. But when he

Fans at Chicago's iconic Wrigley Field couldn't wait for Bryant to make his debut there.

slammed three home runs in the first week, the Cubs knew it was time.

Bryant made his major league debut on April 17 in a game against the San Diego Padres at Chicago's famed Wrigley Field. He had been a dominant hitter wherever he played. He was about to do the same at the highest level of baseball.

CHAPTER 4

SUPERSTAR

Most rookies struggle with their first taste of major league pitching. But Kris Bryant wasn't just any rookie. He simply picked up where he had left off in the minors.

Bryant collected nine hits in his first six games. He hit a double in four straight games. He batted .318 in April.

It didn't take Bryant long to adjust to life in the big leagues.

And he began launching long home runs. The big blast became his **trademark**.

Bryant did more than just hit. Cubs manager Joe Maddon praised Bryant for his all-around play. The rookie performed well at third base. He ran the bases like a veteran. He showed better speed than most people expected from a player his size. And he hustled from the beginning to the end of every game.

The Cubs relied on Bryant to play like a veteran, and he didn't let them down. He socked two home runs on a July 4 win against the Miami Marlins. One was a **grand slam** that broke the game open.

Bryant celebrates his first major league home run on May 9, 2015, at Milwaukee's Miller Park.

He finished second on the team in hits, home runs, and runs batted in (RBIs).

Bryant hit .316 with 19 RBIs in September as the team nailed down a playoff spot. Then he helped the Cubs knock off their archrivals, the St. Louis Cardinals, in the first round of the National League playoffs.

From left, Cubs manager Joe Maddon, first baseman Anthony Rizzo, and Bryant observe the action.

The Cubs eventually lost to the New York Mets in the 2015 NL Championship Series, but the team's future looked bright. Bryant was a big reason for people's optimism. And he was even better in 2016. Bryant hit 39 home runs, which was third most in the NL. He led the league in runs scored. He won the NL Most Valuable Player (MVP) Award. And most importantly, he helped the Cubs snap their 108-year streak without a world championship. That alone will make Kris Bryant a hero in Chicago for a long, long time.

GOING DEEP

Bryant made history in 2016 when he hit three home runs and two doubles in a game against the Cincinnati Reds. He was the first player in MLB history to do that. And he was the youngest player in Cubs history to hit three homers in a game.

KRIS BRYANT

- Height: 6 feet 5 inches (196 cm)
- Weight: 215 pounds (98 kg)
- Birth date: January 4, 1992
- Birthplace: Las Vegas, Nevada
- High school: Bonanza High School, Las Vegas
- College: University of San Diego (2010–2013)
- MLB team: Chicago Cubs (2015–)
- Major awards: Dick Howser Trophy (2013);
    Golden Spikes Award (2013);
    National League Rookie of the Year (2015);
    National League MVP (2016)

Las Vegas

San Diego

Chicago

FOCUS ON
KRIS BRYANT

Write your answers on a separate piece of paper.

1. Write a sentence that describes the key ideas of Chapter 4.

2. Do you think the Cubs kept Kris Bryant in the minor leagues too long? Why or why not?

3. Where did Kris Bryant go to college?
   - A. Las Vegas
   - B. Iowa
   - C. San Diego

4. Why did Kris Bryant go back to Las Vegas after he signed with the Cubs?
   - A. He was playing for a minor league team there.
   - B. He wanted to hang out with his friend Bryce Harper.
   - C. He wanted to help the people in his hometown.

Answer key on page 32.

GLOSSARY

All-American
An honor given to the best players in college sports.

competitive
Having a strong desire to win in a sport or other activity.

draft
A system that allows teams to acquire new players coming into a league.

grand slam
A home run with the bases loaded.

playoffs
A competition to determine a champion in a sport.

selfless
Thinking about and acting for others rather than oneself.

trademark
Talent or skill for which a person is known.

TO LEARN MORE

BOOKS

Castle, George. *Chicago Cubs*. Minneapolis: Abdo Publishing, 2015.

Jacobs, Greg. *The Everything Kids' Baseball Book: From Baseball's History to Today's Favorite Players—with Lots of Home Run Fun in Between*. Avon, MA: Adams Media, 2016.

Nagelhout, Ryan. *20 Fun Facts about Baseball*. New York: Gareth Stevens Publishing, 2016.

NOTE TO EDUCATORS

Visit **www.focusreaders.com** to find lesson plans, activities, links, and other resources related to this title.

INDEX

Answer Key: 1. Answers will vary; **2.** Answers will vary; **3.** C; **4.** C